Bring This Book to Life With Your Phone or Tablet

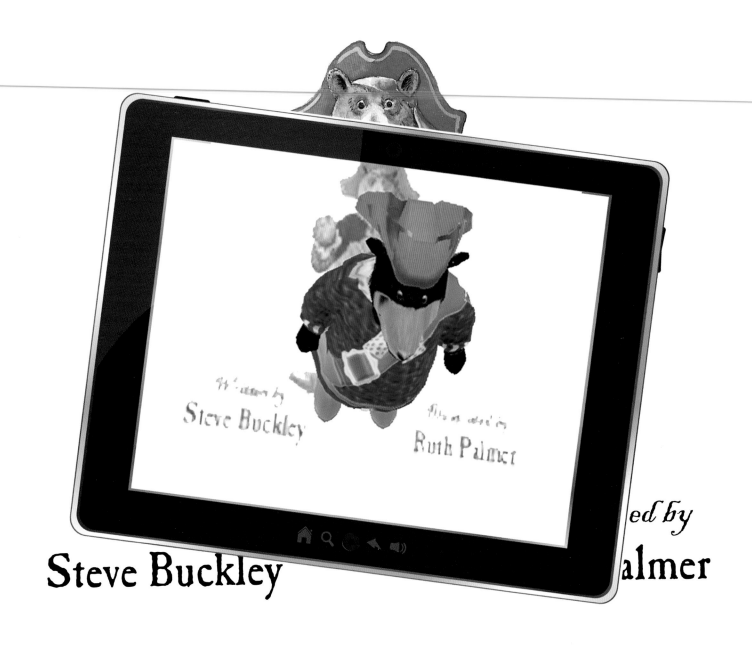

Written by

Steve Buckley

Illustrated by

Ruth Palmer

Steve Buckley

ed by

almer

www.Bangarangbooks.com

Blackbear the Pirate

Written by
Steve Buckley

Illustrated by
Ruth Palmer

More Blackbear the Pirate Adventures:

The Search for Captain Ben
Calico's Ghost

To Learn More About Captain Blackbear and His Crew
Visit www.blackbearthepirate.com

PROMO COPY

Download
FREE App

...ces by combining education and gaming. Edutain-
...d caretakers through fun and engaging technology.

www.Bangarangbooks.com

ISBN 978-0-9821151-2-1 case bound
ISBN 978-1-936818-01-3 e-pub
ISBN 978-1-936818-02-0 e-pdf

Library of Congress Control Number: 2009924403

SeaStory Press
305 Whitehead St. #1
Key West, Florida 33040
www.seastorypress.com

For Katie, Brad, Stephanie & Danielle
So that you may never grow up,
& I may never grow old.

"Ahoy there maties!" said Blackbear the Pirate.

"Ahoy Captain Blackbear!" replied the crew.

"Prepare to set sail!" commanded Blackbear.

"Aye Aye, Captain," said Izzy Paws, the first mate,

"Where we be a heading?"

"We head south," responded Blackbear,

"To the island of Bearataria."

"Hold on there Capt'n, do ye mean to say, Bearataria?" inquired Calico, the saltiest seabear in Blackbear's crew.

"BEARATARIA" squawked Pauly the Parrot, as he sat upon Calico's shoulder.

"Not Bearataria!" exclaimed Bonnie, one of the two girls that sailed the seas with Blackbear.

"I'm not sure I like this idea," grumbled Barty, the oldest and wisest member of the crew.

"I smell adventure a brewing," whispered Izzy to Blackbear.

"Weigh anchor and get us under way, Mr. Paws!" ordered Blackbear the Pirate.

The anchor was raised as Blackbear and his faithful crew set sail aboard the Annie, Blackbear's grand pirate ship.

"Why are we going to Bearataria?" asked Le-Kidd, the youngest member of the crew.

"We go in search of the cave of the great Pirate King, Bearfoot," explained Blackbear.

"Aye there Capt'n, do ye mean to say we seek the cave of Bearfoot?" questioned Calico.

"BEARFOOT!" squawked Pauly the Parrot.

"What if I do not wish to meet the Pirate King, Bearfoot?" asked Bonnie?

"I don't think this is a very good idea," muttered Barty.

"I smell a quarrel a brewing," whispered Izzy to Blackbear.

"We seek a great adventure," said Blackbear, "So we go to Bearataria to find the cave of the great Pirate King, Bearfoot."

As they sailed across the deep blue sea the clouds grew dark and the waves grew rough as wind and rain tossed the Annie about upon the sea.

"Aye there Capt'n, me thinks we should bring the Annie about, and go back!" shouted Calico.

"GO BACK!" squawked Pauly the Parrot.

"The Sea is getting too rough!" exclaimed Bonnie.

"I think I'm going to be sick!" moaned Le-Kidd.

"I knew that this was not a good idea," griped Barty.

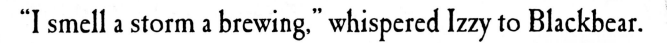

"I smell a storm a brewing," whispered Izzy to Blackbear.

"Batten down the hatches and secure the deck!" ordered Blackbear.

Blackbear the Pirate was a very good captain, and he guided the Annie through the raging wind and rain until the storm had passed.

"Aye there Capt'n, are ye sure ye don't need some sort of map so's we don't get lost?" demanded Calico.

"GET LOST!" squawked Pauly the Parrot.

"How much longer until we see land?" inquired Bonnie.

"Are we lost?" asked Le-Kidd.

"How about if we come up with a new idea," suggested Barty.

"I smell a mutiny a brewing," whispered Izzy to Blackbear.

"Belay that talk!" commanded Blackbear, "In the morning we arrive at Bearataria."

Blackbear the Pirate was a great leader, and he led his crew as they began to climb to the top of Bearface Rock.

"This looks awfully steep to me!" whined Le-Kidd.

"Aye there Capt'n, me thinks it be about time we be heading back to the Annie," suggested Calico.

"BACK TO THE ANNIE!" squawked Pauly the Parrot.

"I'm afraid I'm going to fall," worried Bonnie.

"This is just one bad idea after another!" complained Barty.

"I smell trouble a brewing," whispered Izzy to Blackbear.

"Look!" shouted Blackbear, "We have made it to the top of Bearface Rock."

Blackbear the Pirate was a bold pirate, and after taking his crew to the top of Bearface Rock they came before a dark and menacing cave.

"Arrrhhhg!" came a booming voice from inside the cave,

"Who goes there?"

"What wa-wa-was that?" stuttered Le-Kidd.

"Aye there Capt'n, are ye believing we need to be a going into that cave?" asked Calico.

"INTO THAT CAVE!" squawked Pauly the Parrot.

"I'm not taking one step closer to that cave!" assured Bonnie.

"Going into that cave would be the worst idea ever!" declared Barty.

"I smell danger a brewing," whispered Izzy to Blackbear.

"It is I, Blackbear the Pirate, and my crew," proclaimed Blackbear, "We sailed here aboard my ship, the Annie."

"Why?" demanded the voice, "Why did you cross the stormy seas to come to Bearataria, and why did you face the danger of climbing Bearface Rock to stand before the cave of the great Pirate King, Bearfoot?"

Blackbear the Pirate was a clever pirate, and he knew it was time to show his crew that he was true to his words.

"Why?" replied Blackbear as he looked upon his crew, "We came in search of great adventure, of course, and I believe we found it."

With that, the crew all smiled and said "Aye Captain, we did, this was indeed a great adventure."

With their quest behind them, Blackbear the Pirate and his faithful crew went back to the Annie to set sail in search of their next GREAT ADVENTURE.

"Hey, where did everybody go?" wondered Bearfoot.